FIND THE ANIMAL
GOD MADE
SOMETHING QUICK

This zebra knows what animal we are looking for. Can you find this zebra in the book?

WRITTEN BY PENNY REEVE
ILLUSTRATED BY ROGER DE KLERK

 Published by Christian Focus Publications

Let's go on an adventure, what will we find? It is something that God has made. It is something quick!

Can you find the buffalo?

Come quickly to help me God.
Psalm 22:19

Where is the grey mouse?

What was that? It is a tail. How many tails can you see? God gave this animal a quick moving tail.

Can you find the parrots?

Listen to me and answer me quickly when I call.
Psalm 102:2

Who is wearing green boots?

What is this? It's a claw. How many claws can you see? God made these claws sharp and quick for climbing up trees.

Can you find the giraffe?

When you call to God for help he will say, 'Here I am.' Isaiah 58:9

Where is the pink and yellow bird?

What about this? It's an eye winking at you. How many eyes can you see? God made these eyes small and quick at seeing things.

Can you find the zebra?

God is merciful and quick to forgive.
Isaiah 55:7

Where is the green water bottle?

Can you see the tiny pink tongue? Who else has a tongue in this picture? This little tongue is going quickly out and quickly in. God made this tongue for testing the air.

Can you find the parrot?

The great day of the Lord is very near and coming fast. Zephaniah 1:14

Who is wearing a red hat?

Which animal have we found? It is something quick. It is a lizard. Who made it? Our great God!

Can you find the piece of bread?

For in just a little while God is coming and he will come without delay. Hebrews 10:37

Who is wearing a blue shirt?

Lizards move fast. Their legs move very quickly. But our God is so different. He is everywhere at once!

Can you find the snake?

'My righteousness comes speedily. My salvation is on the way,' says the Lord. Isaiah 51:5

Where is the black and white zebra?

Thank you God for being so quick.
You are everywhere. You always hear and answer my prayers.

Jesus said, "I will be with you always, even to the very end."
Matthew 28:20